To Danny & Harry, the most flatulent people we know —T. F. & D. P.
For Codie —G. P.

ALADDIN

An imprint of Simon & Schuster Children's Publishing Division

1230 Avenue of the Americas, New York, New York 10020

This Aladdin hardcover edition September 2017

Copyright © 2013 by Tom Fletcher and Dougie Poynter

Illustrations by Garry Parsons

Originally published in Great Britain in 2013 by Red Fox.

Published by arrangement with Penguin Random House Children's UK

All rights reserved, including the right of reproduction in whole or in part in any form.

ALADDIN and related logo are registered trademarks of Simon & Schuster, Inc.

For information about special discounts for bulk purchases, please contact
Simon & Schuster Special Sales at 1-866-506-1949 or business@simonandschuster.com.

The Simon & Schuster Speakers Bureau can bring authors to your live event. For more information or to book an event
contact the Simon & Schuster Speakers Bureau at 1-866-248-3049 or visit our website at www.simonspeakers.com.

Manufactured in China 0617 SCP

10 9 8 7 6 5 4 3 2 1

Library of Congress Control Number 2016962347

ISBN 978-1-4814-9866-1 (hc)

ISBN 978-1-4814-9867-8 (eBook)

THE DINOSAUR THAT POOPED A PLANET!

THE DINOSAUR THAT POOPED A PLANET!

Tom Fletcher & Dougie Poynter
Illustrated by Garry Parsons

ALADDIN

NEW YORK LONDON TORONTO SYDNEY NEW DELHI

Danny and Dinosaur liked to have fun.
Some days they had lots, some days they had none.

One day they were bored; they had no games to play.
Danny said, "Dinosaur, what shall we do today?
We could mow the lawn. We could clean up the place.
We could do our chores or we could go to space!"

"But you mustn't forget to have lunch," Mommy said.
"You cannot have fun unless you've been fed."
So they packed a packed lunch for the Science Museum,
Where rockets were kept if you wanted to see them.

There were hundreds of rockets and spaceship surprises,
Tall ones and small ones of all shapes and sizes.
And one that was ready to launch, with a door
Big enough for a boy and his pet dinosaur.

They ignored all the warnings—they couldn't care less.
They pressed all the things they shouldn't have pressed.

T-minus 5 4 3 2 1 IGNITION!

They started their intergalactic space mission.

They flew higher than houses,
And buildings, and cranes;
Much higher than birds,
Even higher than planes.

"We're in space!" Danny yelled as they floated around.
But the dinosaur's tum made a rumbling sound.

Danny looked at his watch. "Is it time for a snack?"
    Then he looked all around for the dino's lunch pack.
Danny started to panic, then started to worry . . .
    Their lunch was back home 'cause they'd left in a hurry!

So with no food, not even a cheeseburger bun,
A disastrous dinosaur feast had begun.

It gobbled up gadgets and gizmos galore—
    Nothing was safe from the space dinosaur.
Robots and ray guns and blinking red blinkers,
    Eating things thought up by NASA's great thinkers!

It chewed and it chomped on the spaceship controls—
The rocket was dotted with dino tooth holes!
The spaceship was empty. Inside it was bare.
Outside there was space stuff to eat everywhere.

It broke down the door
With a cool ninja chop!
Out in space dinosaurs are
Much harder to stop.

It chomped on the moon like a big chunk of cheese,
    Then shoved even more in its mouth with a squeeze.

It munched on the Martians from Mars and their cats
   (Their cats are like ours, but their cats wear cool hats),
Satellites, Saturn, and six supernovas,
   Shape-shifting saucers and seven space rovers.

It guzzled five gallons of fuel from the tank,
   And Danny's jaw dropped as he watched what it drank!
With a crunch and a crack and a nom-nom-nom-nom,
   In one dino gulp, their rocket was gone!

Now nothing was left—all Danny could see
Was a fat dinosaur where the rocket should be.
And so they were stranded with no way back home,
Just Danny and Dino in space all alone.

Now Danny was crying,

He cried
and he cried,

He cried and his
tears filled his
space suit inside.

Unless they were going
To stay there forever,
The dinosaur needed
To do something clever!

With the feeling of guilt deep down in its gut,
Its brain brewed a plan involving its butt.
It knew there was only one thing it could do.
To get them back home, it needed to . . .

Like a poop-powered rocket the dinosaur flew.
So Dan held on tight; it was all he could do!
It pooped out the robots and ray guns and blinkers—
The things NASA's thinkers thought up were now stinkers!
It pooped out the moon, it pooped out the stars,
It pooped the space rovers and Martians from Mars.

When Danny looked back he could see a poop trail
From far out in space to the dinosaur's tail.
They headed for Earth and they started to orbit.
It pooped on the clouds,
but the clouds just absorbed it.

They flew past the buildings and streets of their town,
Leaving the houses all smelly and brown,
And finally landed back down on the ground.
"Hooray!" Danny cried. "We are home, safe and sound!"

Then Dino looked up to the moon way up high,
    Where a new poopy planet had formed in the sky.
And so Danny agreed with what Mommy said,
    That fun is not fun unless you've been fed.

And just when you thought all the pooping was done,
A Mars cat plopped out of the dinosaur's bum.